For Andrew, Anna and Ruby

First published in 1996 by
University of Western Australia Press
Nedlands, Western Australia 6907
under the Cygnet Books imprint

National Library of Australia
Cataloguing-in-publication entry:

Gray, Nigel, 1941– .
The frog prince.

ISBN 1 875560 68 8.
1 875560 70 X. (pb)

I. Langoulant, Allan. II. Title.

A823.3

Consultant editor: Amanda Curtin,
Curtin Communications, Perth
Designed by Robyn Tomlinson
Typeset in Caslon 3
Printed by South China Printing Co.,
Hong Kong

NIGEL GRAY

ALLAN LANGOULANT

CYGNET BOOKS

here was once
a handsome
prince, and on his
twenty-first birthday
a jealous wizard
cast a spell on him.

And the prince fell asleep for one thousand years.

As time went by,
the prince's castle was abandoned.
It fell into disrepair,
and a thick thicket grew up
all around.

After nine hundred and
ninety-nine years,
a beautiful princess,
out riding one day,
came upon the thick
thicket.
Through it she glimpsed
the ruined castle.

The princess began to hack her way
through the undergrowth and brambles.

Finally she reached the castle doorway.
She gave the old door a mighty karate kick.
Kerpow!
The door swung inwards.
Its rusty hinges broke.
The door fell on
to the floor
with a
dust-raising
crash.

The princess searched the castle.

She poked her
nose into every room.

At last,
in the attic room of a high tower,
she came upon the sleeping prince.
He was still twenty-one
and, though rather dusty,
as handsome as ever.

The wash basin was dry,
so the princess wetted her hanky with spit,
and wiped the dust from the prince's face.
And as she did so, she fell in love.

The princess bent forward
and kissed the prince gently on the lips
to try to waken him.

Sure enough,
the prince woke up.

But what a shock for them both
when he changed instantly into a frog.

"You great twit!"
croaked the frog prince.
"You interfering busybody!
I only had one more year to go,
and then I'd have woken up
and been a handsome prince
again. And now look at me!
A fine mess you've got me into!"

"I'm terribly sorry," said the princess.
"Is there anything I can do to make amends?"

"Well...You could try asking me
to marry you," said the frog prince.
"That sometimes works wonders."

Despite being a princess,
she was a good-hearted girl.
And besides, remembering
how dishy the frog had
been as a prince,
she thought she'd give
it a whirl.
"Dear frog prince," she said,
"will you marry me?"

"Yes," said the frog prince,
"I will."

Then, an amazing
thing happened.

The princess turned into a frog as well.

"Oh, no!" said the frog princess.
"You fool! You idiot! You nincompoop!
Now look what you made me do!"

"Well, it's no good carrying on like that," said the frog prince.

"There must be a way out of this mess."

So they tried proposing to each other. They tried big sloppy kisses.

They tried leap-frogging down the stairs.
But nothing worked.

Finally, her green skin shiny with tears,
the frog princess said,
"It's no good. I'll be a frog forever."

"Well, what can't be cured must be endured,"
said the frog prince.
"But you'll always be a princess to me,
and I will love you till I croak."

"Oh, it's too dry and dusty here,"
whined the frog princess.
"Let's look for somewhere cool and damp and slimy."

So they did.

They hopped out of the old castle, and soon discovered a neglected lilypond in the overgrown garden.

They found it hard to make friends with the other
frogs — because they didn't speak the lingo.
So they stayed together.
And by and by, they had a pond full of tadpoles.

Then one day,
as they sat together on a waterlily leaf,
admiring their growing family —

SHAZAM!

The prince's final year was up,
and he was his old self again.

He lifted the frog princess on the palm of his hand.
"Kiss me!" she begged, in her little froggy voice.
"Don't leave me like this!"

"If I kiss you," said the prince,
"who knows whether
you'll become a princess, or
I'll become a frog."
Then, with a frog in his throat,
he added, "But I guess I'd
rather be a frog with
you than a
prince without
you."

The prince found himself a frog again,
sitting on the princess's palm.
"Oh, no," croaked the prince.

"Never mind," said the princess,
"I still love you, even if you are a frog."

So she took him
home to her palace...

and lived happily ever after.